D0422518

Slimy Salamanders!

by Renee McCuen

Illustrated by David Hemenway

Worthington, Minnesota

For my family:
Bob, Jenny, and Leah

—Renee McCuen

Acknowledgements

Special thanks to Libby Kester for her expertise while showing me her salamanders and answering all of my questions. Ryan Jacobson provided me with all of the support I needed to make this book a reality. Thanks for all your hard work! David Hemenway, your talent is amazing!

Credits

Edited by Ryan Jacobson
Logo design by Shane Nitzsche

ISBN: 978-0-9833667-2-0

10 9 8 7 6 5 4 3 2 1

Contents

DANNY & ESTER

I'm Danny, and I had a problem. My white paper sack was almost empty. There was only one fortune cookie left in the bag. I had already opened all of the others. The fortunes inside kept saying, "You don't need a fortune yet."

Ester's and my adventures always start with a fortune cookie. We found out that we can turn into any animal we want. We just have to say together that the animal is "interesting." The first time we did it, we turned into jellyfish. The next time, we became ants.

4

But first we got fortune cookies at Mr. Lee's restaurant. The fortunes inside were important. They told us what to do as animals in order to turn back into humans.

I was thinking a lot about salamanders, but I needed a good fortune. I wondered what the last cookie would say. It was time to find out.

My fingers fumbled on the wrapper as I worked on opening it. I squeezed my eyes shut and then opened them to read what it said.

Salamanders are interesting!

All right!

I had to get Ester prepared, and I knew just the way to do it. She said she would never turn into an animal again, but this would change her mind . . . I hoped.

1

TIGER

I was sitting on the front steps of our apartment building, thinking about my plan. I thought if Ester saw a salamander for real, she would want to become one.

Footsteps pounded down the stairs. The door squeaked open, and Ester joined me on the steps.

"Here you are," Ester said. "I've been looking all over for you."

"Hi, Ester, I was just on the phone with Libby. She wants to show us something."

"What does she want to show us?"

"She has three amphibians in her basement."

Ester's eyes got big. "Are you talking about snakes and lizards?"

"Lots of people think lizards and snakes are amphibians," I said. "But they aren't. Lizards and snakes are reptiles. All reptiles have dry, scaly skin. Amphibians have moist skin, and most of them start their lives in water. Libby loves amphibians. She says she's going to be a herpetologist when she grows up."

"What is that?" asked Ester.

"It's a scientist who studies amphibians and reptiles," I answered. "Now, let's go. Libby told me we could visit Tiger anytime."

"A tiger!" she gasped.

I laughed. "No, not a tiger. A tiger salamander. It has stripes on its body like a tiger. Libby named it Tiger."

"I'll go with you to look," said Ester.

She grabbed my arm and squeezed it. "I hope you aren't trying to change my mind. I'm never turning into an animal again. It's just too scary."

She sounded sure, so I hoped my idea would change her mind.

2

IN THE BASEMENT

We walked to Libby's house and knocked on the door. Libby opened it and smiled. "Hi, Danny and Ester," she said. "Did you come to visit Tiger? She's in the basement because it's cooler and more humid down there."

Libby led us down the steps. I had to push Ester to get her going.

"How long have you had Tiger?" Ester asked.

"A couple of years," Libby replied. "Salamanders are so interesting."

Ester made a squealing noise.

"Are you okay?" Libby asked.

"Interesting things make me nervous. Isn't that right, Danny?" Ester said.

Libby patted Ester's back. "Come on. I think you'll like Tiger."

She led us to a terrarium. It was kind of like a big fish aquarium, except it wasn't full of water.

"I'll take Tiger out, so you can see her better," Libby said. She washed her hands.

"Why aren't you using soap?" I asked.

"Salamanders have very sensitive skin," Libby said. "Their skin needs to be moist, and our dry hands can hurt them. Soap can hurt them too."

I could tell that Libby had done her research. She worked hard to keep Tiger healthy.

Tiger was black with yellow stripes. She had a long tail and googly eyes on the top of her head, like a frog.

"Look how slowly she moves," said Ester.

Libby put Tiger back, and we watched her for a long time. Libby put a cricket into the terrarium. Tiger stuck out her sticky tongue and gobbled it down.

Ester made a face. I knew she was thinking about a caterpillar she had eaten as an ant. I could tell she liked Tiger, though.

Ester finally washed her hands and touched the salamander. "Her skin is slimy and moist. Why is it that way?"

"The slime tastes gross to other animals," Libby said. "It's actually poison. It protects salamanders from predators."

Ester gently looked Tiger over. After a while, she washed her hands again. She studied a bumpy toad and a tree frog. Those were Libby's other two amphibians.

At last we thanked Libby and headed back to the apartment. As we walked, I heard Ester sigh.

"What's wrong, Ester?"

I was hoping Tiger would have changed Ester's mind. Maybe she was curious. Maybe she wanted to go to the pond to turn into salamanders.

"Nothing," Ester said. "I think it's inter— um, neat that a salamander's skin protects it." She sighed again. "That makes me feel safer. I think we should walk to the pond."

"Really?" I gasped. "Let's go right now!"

We took the long, narrow path to the pond. Both of us were quiet, thinking about salamanders and what it would be like to be one. Then I remembered the fortunes.

"What about the fortunes?" we both said at the same time.

"I looked at the rest of mine. They said, 'You don't need a fortune yet,'" Ester told me.

"Mine said mostly the same thing. What should we do?" I asked.

We decided to try and talk my mother and Ester's mother into taking us to our favorite Chinese restaurant. We would ask Mr. Lee for more cookies. We needed them to find out what our jobs would be as salamanders. When we finished those jobs, we would become human again.

I was so excited. I knew it was going to be hard to sleep that night.

3

FORTUNES

Poisonous, slimy skin keeps most predators away.

I looked at the strange fortune, and shivers of excitement tingled down my spine. I was with the Sanchez family and my mother at our favorite restaurant, Lee's Chinese Palace. I was waiting for Ester to finish eating. She kept stuffing food in her mouth, even though everyone else was done.

Mrs. Sanchez laughed and said, "Ester, you must be starving today. I've never seen you eat so much."

Ester whispered at me through the food in her mouth. "I want to be so full that I won't eat anything else until supper tonight. I really don't want to eat any muddy creatures."

She finally finished and picked up her fortune cookie. She took a deep breath and opened it. She scrunched up her face and shivered like I had. Except she didn't look excited. She looked scared.

"What does it say?" I asked.

She shook her head and handed me the slip of paper. I looked at the crumpled piece of paper. It said, *Learn how to swim.*

I didn't see a problem with that. I love to swim. "It's a good idea, Ester. You should learn."

Ester gave me a nasty look. "You know I don't like the water."

It was almost time to go, but we had not seen Mr. Lee, the restaurant owner. I got up to peek in the kitchen. He wasn't there. Mom was still chatting with Mrs. Sanchez. I motioned for Ester to come with me. We looked in his office. He wasn't there. So we stopped in the kitchen to ask Mrs. Lee, a short woman with long, black hair.

"Where is Mr. Lee?" I was starting to worry.

Mrs. Lee said, "He was in the pantry, but I think he's working at the cash register now."

We hurried to the cash register, and sure enough, there he was. He grinned at us. "Your mothers are looking for you. They are waiting outside." He brushed his hands against his white apron.

"Mr. Lee," said Ester. "We need more fortunes."

He reached under the counter and took out two white bags. "Is it time for another adventure? I put these here, just in case." He handed us the bags. "Enjoy! You'll have to tell me about your adventures some time." He turned to help another customer.

"Thank you, Mr. Lee. You're the best," we yelled as we ran out the door.

4

OH, NO!

"See you later, Mom," I said. "Ester and I are going to the pond. We're going to be— I mean, we're going to look for salamanders."

I skipped down the steps. The bag in my hand bumped against my leg.

Ester was waiting by the sidewalk. "Danny, tell me more about salamanders. I want to know what to expect when we get to the pond."

"Salamanders, frogs and toads are amphibians," I told her. "Amphibian means 'double life.' They usually hatch from eggs and live in the water. When

20

they are born, they breathe with gills just like fish. As they grow up, most amphibians develop lungs. They need to breathe air just like we do. Most amphibians live the second part of their lives on land."

We stopped by the edge of the pond.

"Adult salamanders are hard to spot," I said. "After they leave the pond, they spend most of their time underground. Salamanders need moist skin. They have glands under their skin that make mucus to keep them moist. Other glands make poisons that help keep them safe from predators."

Ester giggled. "When I had a cold one time, your mom told me I was full of mucus. I think that's a polite name for snot."

Wild grasses and cattails rustled in the breeze. It was spring, so we could hear frogs croaking for their mates. The pond was a good habitat for amphibians.

"Are you ready?" I asked Ester.

"No, Danny! I need more time. Tell me more about salamanders before we change. "

"Okay, there are lots of different kinds of salamanders. The largest is the Chinese Giant Salamander. It can grow to be five feet long. It's so big, it can eat ducks."

"Wow, that's big!" said Ester.

"Some salamanders live in caves. Their skin is white, and they are blind because their eyes are below a layer of their skin. The Blue Spotted Salamander can walk over ice and snow to lay eggs in frigid ponds. Oh, and the Iberian Ribbed Newt has sharp ribs that can stick through its skin to poke animals trying to attack it."

"Sort of like a porcupine," Ester noted.

She shook her white bag. "I'll go first." She picked three cookies and ripped them open. She looked quickly at each one and then threw them on the ground.

"What do they say?" I asked.

"They each say I should learn to swim." She stamped her foot. "I'll go in the water, but I won't learn how to swim. I'll just stay near the shore."

"Salamanders are great swimmers. You might enjoy it."

Ester glared at me again as I chose my three fortunes.

Explore the pond.

Tunnel in for a little rest.

Those seemed simple enough. I already wanted to explore the pond. Salamanders dig tunnels or even live in small, deserted tunnels most of their adult lives. That would be easy to do.

Lose a part of yourself to become human again.

What!

What did that mean? Did it mean I would lose something that wouldn't matter, like some hair? Or did it mean I would lose my arm or leg?"

5

"INTERESTING"

I changed my mind. I did not want to be a
salamander anymore!

"Let's go, Danny. I'm ready. We both have to say
it at the same time, or we won't change."

She was right. If we both said a creature was
interesting, we would turn into that creature and
learn about it. I had wanted to find out about
salamanders, until I read the fortune.

Ester grabbed my hand and started saying,
"Salamanders are so interesting."

I said, "Salamanders . . ." And then I stopped.

I needed to tell her what the fortune said. I couldn't change. It was too dangerous.

I felt something funny and sticky on my hand. I was going to shake it off, when I noticed Ester wasn't standing by me. I looked down and saw four soft, slimy little fingers grasping my hand. It was Ester! She had changed, but I had not. Her salamander mouth was opening and closing. She was talking to me, but I couldn't understand her.

I set her gently on the ground and sat down beside her. She looked mostly like a salamander. She looked a bit like herself too. Her large, brown eyes stared up at me. Her long, black hair hung in a neat braid down her back.

Last time, we had a good laugh because we looked so strange. This time it wasn't funny. I didn't know what to do.

"I'm so sorry, Ester." I told her.

EXPLORE THE POND

She stomped her feet and lashed her tail back and forth.

I looked at her and knew what I had to do. I talked her into doing this. And she would never be human again if I didn't change and follow the fortunes.

I took a deep breath, touched her salamander hand and said, "Salamanders are so interesting."

"Danny, what just happened? I was so scared when you didn't change," she sobbed.

I looked down at my black body with yellow stripes. I gulped and told Ester what the fortune had said.

Her wide mouth frowned. "We'll have to be very careful, Danny."

That was a good idea. Now that I was a salamander, I wasn't quite so worried. We would follow the fortunes, learn, and then change back.

29

6

IN THE POND

"We need to explore the pond," I said.

That's what my fortune was. I actually couldn't wait to get in the water.

"Are you sure? I know you're a good swimmer, but I can't really even float very well. Deep water makes me panic," Ester told me.

"That won't be a problem," I said. "Salamanders are good swimmers. Remember, they begin their lives in the water."

We walked to the edge of the pond, and I went into the water headfirst.

I always jump right in when we go to the pool. Ester doesn't like cold water so she goes in, little by little. First she gets her feet in. Then she inches in a little more. Next she goes up to her knees. It seems like it takes her forever.

She was no different as a salamander. She put her front toes in and just stood there.

"Come on, Ester! The water's great."

"I will. Just give me a few minutes," she said.

Her legs went in and then her belly. At last she was in the pond. I paddled back and forth, waiting for her. I was so excited that I forgot to be careful.

"I'll race you to that branch," I yelled, and I took off. I swished my tail as I swam underwater. I sure could move fast. I only had to come up for a quick breath one time.

"Beat you!" I said when I reached the branch. I looked back to see how far she was behind me.

I couldn't see her! She wasn't by the edge of the pond. She wasn't by the branch, and I didn't see her anywhere in between.

7

WHERE'S ESTER?

My mind started racing. What if Ester was still a bad swimmer? Why did I leave her behind? I should have checked on her before I started the race. I knew she was nervous.

I dove and thrashed through the pond. "Ester, Ester! Where are you?"

I swam this way and that, searching for her. I couldn't see her. I climbed onto a large, flat rock to look over the pond.

A snapping turtle was under the water, and something was hanging from his powerful jaws. It was something small, but it looked like a tail—a salamander tail.

"No!" I screamed and dove in. "We're supposed to be poisonous. Don't you know that?" I headed straight for the turtle. I got close to him and saw exactly what was clamped in his mouth.

A frog.

Relief rushed through me, but not for long. This turtle didn't care that I was poisonous. It started to chase me. Turtles are slow on land. They're not slow in the water!

I had seen what those powerful jaws could do. I swam away as fast as I could. I flipped my tail and paddled hard. It didn't help. The turtle followed, snapping at me.

I was barely keeping ahead of him. He didn't need to come up for air as often as I did. I slowed down when I went to the surface. Every time I did

that, the turtle got closer. And I was getting tired, oh, so tired.

I spied some dead leaves near the bottom of the pond and ducked under them. Maybe the turtle wouldn't be able to see me.

I held my breath until I thought I would burst. I waited and waited until I ran out of air. Then I moved, hoping the turtle had given up. That was when something grabbed me from behind.

8

DIRTY BELLIES

I squirmed and wiggled with my tail and legs. That turtle wasn't going to get me without a fight.

"Danny, stop!" said a familiar voice. Ester stared at me with worried eyes. "I thought you were going to be careful." She pushed me out of the pond. "That turtle looked dangerous. It kept following you until you slipped under the leaves.

"Where were you? I looked all over. I must have called your name a hundred times." I shuddered, thinking about the turtle and how I thought it had eaten her.

"I just stayed here with my head under the water. I was looking at the water bugs and rocks. I didn't hear you, but I saw you hide under those leaves. Then you didn't come up. I was so worried about you!"

Salamanders don't have eardrums. So they don't hear the way we do. They pick up vibrations through their legs. Ester and I were lucky we could talk and hear while in animal form.

We decided that we would stick together from now on. That way, we could help each other if one of us got into trouble.

The turtle was gone, so I swam out a short way. I called for Ester to join me. After a bit, she found that swimming was easy in her salamander body.

We explored the pond in the shining sun. We saw water plants swaying. Small frogs darted through the water.

The sunlight warmed the water, and the water warmed us. People are warm-blooded, but amphibians are ectothermic. That means they are cool when their surroundings are cool and warm when their surroundings are warm.

A salamander larva swam by. It was a baby salamander. It looked a lot like a grown salamander, but it had gills that looked like feathers. So it didn't need to go up for air. It got its oxygen from the water, just like fish do.

"Danny, that was amazing. There was so much to see! I kept swishing my tail, and I could really swim. I'm going to ask my mom if I can take swim lessons. I probably won't ever swim as well this, but I really want to learn."

We got out of the water to explore on land. We had not gone far when I heard Ester moaning behind me.

"My tummy is dragging in the mud," she wailed. We're so low to the ground. My belly is getting dirty. So is my braid!"

She was right. Salamanders have short legs. My hair didn't look so orange now. Parts of it were covered with mud.

"We might be messy, but it feels cool and good." I wiggled in the mud a little more. "This is great!"

"No, it isn't. It feels gross," she said.

Then Ester said she remembered what our third grade teacher, Mrs. Roos, had said: "Scientists don't say gross or ick. They say that things are interesting."

"I mean, it feels interesting," Ester added. "But interesting in a way that I don't like."

She rubbed her face with her short little fingers, but then she saw something move. She followed it away from the pond.

"Hey, wait," I said. "Where are you going?"

9

GUMMY WORMS

"Do you see that earthworm? It looks huge. Probably because we're so small," Ester said.

She walked closer to it. Then, all of a sudden, she opened her large mouth and stuck out her sticky tongue. She gobbled up the worm. She was busy swallowing when she got a sick look on her face.

She began to chant, "Gummy worm. Gummy worm. Gummy worm."

It sounded a little bit like, "Gmm wmm, gmm wmm, gmm wmm," because her mouth was full.

When she was done swallowing, she looked at me with a puzzled look on her face.

"I ate lunch. I made sure I was full. But that worm looked so good. I just had to have it for dessert." Her voice got kind of screechy. "I just ate a worm! I think maybe it was crammed full of dirt. That's what worms eat, isn't it?"

"Yes," I told her.

"When it was in my mouth, I tried to imagine that it was a gummy worm. It was kind of stretchy and chewy."

I decided to make her feel better. I saw another worm. My sticky tongue shot out and caught it. The worm was stretchy and chewy, like Ester said. It didn't taste too bad.

"Salamanders also eat snails and insects," I added. "Tiger salamanders are large amphibians. So they can eat small frogs and even baby mice."

"Danny, please stop me from going near any more food!" said Ester. "I especially don't want to eat a mouse. It would be furry. It has a slinky tail and those little clawed feet. You know, that sounds kind of yummy. So I mean it. Don't let me eat again!"

10

CAUGHT BY A CAT

The sun was directly overhead. We were starting to get hot—too hot. We moved even farther away from the pond.

"Here are some wet leaves." Ester said, "Let's climb under them. I need to cool down."

"My fortune said we should tunnel in for a little rest. It feels good under these leaves. It will feel even better in a burrow, an underground tunnel."

Ester frowned. "I don't know about that. It will be dark, and we won't be able to see."

"We won't have to stay for long," I told her.

Ester nodded.

"Let's find a burrow nearby. Salamanders can dig, but that might take too long. Our moms won't be happy if we don't get home soon."

I turned and walked through the grass, looking for a tunnel to rest in. I was so busy looking that I didn't notice Ester freeze beside me.

"Danny," she whispered. "It's a cat. Do you think she knows we're poisonous?"

I looked up. The cat's body was crouched. Her eyes were staring right at us.

"Run!" I shouted. "Head for the pile of leaves."

I should have known better. There was no way a salamander could outrun a cat. The cat pounced. I felt claws snag my tail.

"She's got me," I said. "Run, Ester!"

Ester turned to run, but then she got a stubborn look in her eyes.

"I'm coming to rescue you!" she yelled.

She ran toward the cat. The cat tightened its grip on me. I knew I was a goner. I kept trying to run, but I could not get away.

Then, all of a sudden, my tail popped off!

11

THE LAST JOB

I forgot. Salamanders can lose their tails when they are in danger. I ran for it. "Come on, Ester!" I yelled.

We scooted, trying to get as far away as we could. The cat was still playing with the tail, hitting it back and forth.

Ester and I didn't stop running until we ran out of breath.

"Are you okay?" asked Ester. She walked around me, checking me over.

I nodded. "I'm fine. Just tired from running."

She looked at the spot where my tail used to be. "Does it hurt?" she asked.

"No, not really," I told her. Then I said, "You were so brave, Ester. Thanks for coming to help me."

I was glad salamanders can regenerate body parts. That means they can grow legs, feet and tails that fall off.

"Hey, the fortune," I remembered. "I lost part of myself. It was just like the fortune said. And that wasn't so bad."

"Not so bad!" Ester screamed. "It was horrible, and we're not even done yet. We still need to find a burrow or tunnel. And that cat is still nearby."

She stopped talking and huffed at me. I had never seen her so mad before. I needed to find a burrow, so she would calm down.

I saw a hole by a bush. It seemed like a good place to rest. I looked carefully. Yes, it was just right.

I started to crawl in. "Follow me, Ester."

The ground was moist and cool. It felt great. We were surrounded by earth. I started feeling sleepy, but Ester poked me with her stubby fingers. I tried to ignore her, but she poked me again.

"Danny, I don't like this. There's dirt and mud all around. It's all over my skin!"

I could hear the panic in Ester's voice. I liked the burrow, but I had to respect her feelings. We needed to move.

"Back out," I said. "You'll be fine. Pretend it's the mud mask your mom puts on her face. She says it's good for her skin."

Ester sighed with relief when we reached the surface. "I didn't like that. When we were ants, the tunnels were bigger. This burrow was too small. I could feel the sides touching me."

"I bet you wouldn't like to hibernate all winter, like salamanders do," I said.

"You're right," she answered.

We waited beside the bush. We were done with our jobs. It was time to become kids again.

Ester poked me and squealed, "Danny, look! There's the cat again."

It was crouched, staring at us. Its muscles bunched, and then it leaped.

12

COVERED IN MUD

We screamed as the cat landed on top of us. She hissed at us, and her claws dug into my . . . jeans?

Yes! We were kids again.

The cat took one look at us and whimpered. Then she turned and ran off. We were saved.

Ester rolled over and looked at me. She had a shocked look on her face. "First that cat pulled off your tail. Then it attacked us again. I thought tasting gross would keep us safe, but no!" She looked at me and asked, "Are you okay? You're not missing an arm or leg, are you?"

I checked myself. I still had both legs and both arms. I seemed to be in one piece. I smiled and said, "I feel great."

"Danny, I am never doing that again," Ester snapped. She stood up, ready to run home.

We heard Hector, Ester's brother, calling for us. "Hey niños where are you?" he yelled.

"Down by the pond," we called back.

We heard the grass rustling and saw Hector walking toward us.

"Mama says it's time to come in."

He looked at us, and his mouth fell open. "Ester, what is it with you? Danny is always messy but not you. Why are you covered in mud?" He bent to brush some off her cheek. "Yuck, Ester, you have worm breath."

He pinched his nose and started for home. But he spotted a salamander larva swimming in the

water. "Cool," he said. "I think I'll take you home with me." He bent down to pick it up.

Ester poked him. "Leave it alone! It has gills. It can't breathe out of water. Your dry hands will hurt it. Besides, it will be much happier here at the pond."

They watched the salamander swim away.

"Okay," Hector said. "Come on, niños. You better go clean up. You are late for supper."

We went back to the apartment. I was thinking about our adventure. Don't tell Ester, but I was also thinking about opossums.

Also check out:

Amazing
Ants!

For more information, visit
www.ReneeMcCuen.com

A Pet Salamander

My friend's daughter, Libby, has five salamanders. Libby and her mother say salamanders are easy pets to keep. But owning a pet is also a big responsibility. Libby takes excellent care of her salamanders.

Here are some things to know about salamanders before choosing one as a pet:

1. It's best to find a pet store that sells captive-bred salamanders. Taking them from the wild can harm them and their environment.

2. Salamanders can live up to 25 years. It's a big job caring for a pet for that long. Be sure that you are willing to take on the responsibility.

3. You will have to handle insects and worms to feed your salamander.

4. Salamanders can carry diseases, so you must always wash your hands after touching your pet.

5. The equipment needed to care for a salamander can cost a lot of money.

Are you still thinking about having a salamander as a pet? Here's what else you will need:
- *A cool, humid room for your terrarium*
- *Potting soil (without vermiculite) and sphagnum moss that can be kept moist to allow burrowing*
- *Rocks or plants for hiding places*

You should also get a good book on how to care for your new pet. Enjoy observing and learning about your salamander.

About the Author

Renee McCuen has enjoyed working with children as an elementary school teacher for 34 years. Her favorite subject is science.

Just like in the story, her students learned to never say, "Gross," or, "Ick." Instead they would say, "Interesting," because everything in the world is indeed interesting.

We have creatures big and small living in our neighborhoods and sometimes even in our houses. Renee hopes *Danny & Ester's Fortunate Adventures* will help you to learn about some of these creatures and to be curious about the others you see.

Renee lives in Worthington, Minnesota, with her husband, Bob, who buys her microscopes and rocks, and listens to all of her "interesting" facts.